Jill Esbaum

Pictures by Roger Roth

Farrar Straus Giroux • New York

For Dana, Tyler, Brett, and Kerri, who make life fun and home the best place to be   —J.E.

For my wonderful big brother, Rob Roth, who used to let me watch him draw   —R.R.

Text copyright © 2004 by Jill Esbaum
Illustrations copyright © 2004 by Roger Roth
All rights reserved
Distributed in Canada by Douglas & McIntyre Ltd.
Color separations by Chroma Graphics PTE Ltd.
Printed and bound in the United States of America by Phoenix Color Corporation
Designed by Nancy Goldenberg
First edition, 2004
10 9 8 7 6 5 4 3 2 1

Library of Congress Cataloging-in-Publication Data
Esbaum, Jill.
    Stink soup / Jill Esbaum ; pictures by Roger Roth.— 1st ed.
      p.   cm.
    Summary: When Annabelle and her brother go to stay with their
grandmother, Annabelle tries to keep him out of trouble, struggles to
avoid eating the tomatoes she hates, and has an encounter with a skunk.
    ISBN 0-374-37252-7
    [1. Tomatoes—Fiction.   2. Brothers and sisters—Fiction.   3. Grandmothers—
Fiction.   4. Farm life—Fiction.]   I. Roth, Roger, ill.   II. Title.

PZ7.E74458 St 2004
[E]—dc21
                                                     2002021605

Granny's chickens stood petrified, staring at my brother with shiny button eyes. He drummed the car door again and yelled, "Buk-BAWWWWK!"

. . . and feathers flew as the whole herd lit out for the coop like their tails were on fire.

"Willie," Mama said fretfully, "you behave."

"Yes, Mama," said Willie.

But Mama and I both knew Willie wasn't too good at following orders. Her eyes met mine in the rearview mirror. "Annabelle, you keep your brother out of trouble . . . promise me, now."

"I promise," I said, holding tighter to his overalls.

Mama sighed real big.

Granny crushed me to her faded blouse. She smelled like sunshine and lavender bath powder and wore a skirt that swished around her ankles.

"For gardenin'," she said, showing it off to Mama. "So's I can bend down without scarin' the mailman."

They both laughed.

Not me. Mama'd volunteered me to help Granny put up the garden, and I knew what that meant: lots of hard work.

Mama left, and Granny led me to the shady side of the porch. She eyed me sideways as I gawked at a red tomato mountain.

"You ready?"

"Ready as I'll ever be," I squeaked through a throat gone tight. Granny tied an apron around me while I watched my brother escape to the barn. Willie was staying for the week, too.

To play.

"First off, they gotta be clean," Granny said, parking me beside an
old washtub. "Then put 'em in this here bucket. When it's full, bring it
in to me."

Well, far as I'm concerned, the only good tomato is a gone tomato.
But washing them didn't sound so bad. Course, the job would have been
easier if I hadn't promised Mama I'd keep Willie out of trouble.

It was a promise easier made than kept. Willie and trouble went
together like biscuits and gravy.

I'd barely started the tomatoes when I heard a crash from the barn.

I ran over and squinted into the gloom. "Willie?"

"Watch out, Annabelle!"

Willie blurred past, spinning me into dusty hay bales.

None too happy about pulling that heavy cart, Chester whirled and twisted and bucked all the way across the barnyard—while Willie hung on like a rodeo cowboy.

I chased them through the pasture, over lumps and bumps and cow patties . . .

"Stop, Chester!" I yelled. "Stop!"

I couldn't catch up till they hit the creek. And I mean *hit*.

Granny came bounding across the lumps and bumps and cow patties, her skirt hitched up around her knees.

"For shame, Annabelle!" she scolded. "Poor Chester. Poor Willie."

She untangled *poor* Chester while *poor* Willie hobbled in circles, unable to remember which leg he was supposed to be favoring.

Granny hugged the stuffing out of him.

"Keep an eye on him, Annabelle," she said. "I can't be a-runnin' out here every five minutes."

Willie showed me his tongue.

"I'll sure *try*, Granny," I said.

I wasn't about to make any more promises.

Half an hour later, Willie was lassoing chickens.

Then I caught him paddling in the pond . . .

climbing the windmill . . .

pestering Chester (again) . . .

By the end of the afternoon, I was as wore down as Granny's teeth.
I was mighty relieved when she poked her head out the window and
called, "YOOOOO-HOOOOO! Suppertime!"

I made a beeline for the kitchen.

Granny whacked a skillet onto the table and said, "Y'all are in for a treat."

She whipped off the lid, and my insides gave a leap.

Stewed tomatoes.

I sprang for the door like a grasshopper. "I better find Willie."

Willie was behind the barn, painting a muddy bull's-eye on its back wall.

In a real sweet voice, I said, "Come to supper, brother dear. We're in for a treat."

I danced a jig back to the house. Wait till Willie saw the main course.

But my little brother was just full of surprises.
Thankfully, Chester wasn't as picky as me.

When Granny told Willie it was bedtime, he didn't even argue. She
gave him another rib-crushing.

"What a *good* boy," she said.

A good boy? Willie wasn't any such thing. He was just pooped. So
was I, but . . . Granny still had *bushels* of cut-up tomatoes waiting to be
squished. She needed help. And there was nobody around but me.

"I'm not tired yet, Granny," I fibbed, hiding a yawn.

I muscled hot red mush through an old strainer.

I shook in salt and pepper and stood back as Granny poured the speckled juice into jars.

Steamy clouds, heavy with the smell of cooked tomatoes, curled from the canner . . . while my stomach dipped and rolled like a slug on a Tilt-A-Whirl.

"My stomach's not feeling so good," I told Granny.

"How's about a little tomato juice?" she asked, rubbing my back. "It's good for what ails ya—"

"M-maybe tomorrow," I said.

I almost told Granny then. I almost said, "Granny, I can't *stand* tomatoes." But the words stuck in my throat.

She was eyeing those shiny jars so proudly.

It was way after midnight when Granny sent me upstairs. Mama's old bed was wide as the Mississippi and soft as dandelion fluff, but no matter. Worrying about that tomato juice kept me awake a long, *long* time.

Sharing the bed with Willie didn't help, either.

Next morning, when I woke up, my heart cartwheeled—Willie was nowhere in sight!

"He went to gather eggs," Granny said. "But he's been out there pert near an hour."

"I'll find him," I said.

Finding Willie wasn't easy. He wasn't lassoing chickens. He wasn't paddling in the pond. Or climbing the windmill. Or pestering Chester . . .

No sir.

He was behind the barn again, pitching eggs at the bull's-eye!

I snatched the basket away.

Just then Granny came wheeling around the corner. She eyed those eggs, smashed to smithereens—and me, standing there with the basket.

I knew how it looked. "Granny, I didn't—"

"I *told* her she'd get a whoopin', Granny," Willie piped up hopefully.

Granny looked at me. She looked at Willie. Then she sighed real big and said, "Well, I ain't never been one to cry over spilt milk."

What about smashed eggs? I wanted to say. But I held my tongue. I figured maybe Granny didn't have the energy to whoop *anybody* after cooking tomatoes all night.

"Take those eggs to the cellar where it's cool," she told Willie.

I glared at his skinny back all the way to the big flat doors set in the ground beside the house.

"And don't forget to shut the doors!" Granny called after him.

The smell of Granny's cinnamon rolls lured me back to the kitchen.
But I'd no more than settled into my chair and reached for one when—
thwoop!—Granny popped the lid on a brand-new jar of tomato juice.
My stomach lurched when she reached for my glass. It was now or
never. I had to speak up—or else choke down that blasted stuff. Sweat
prickled my forehead . . . I took a deep breath . . .

And Granny's head snapped up. "What was that?"

We all listened hard. *Clank.* A sound came from below the floor . . .
like a bucket tipping.

"Willie . . ." Granny said slowly, "did you remember to shut the
cellar doors?"

Willie stirred his eggs in circles. "Yes, Granny."

He was *lying*! It was plain as the eggs on his chin.

Granny tiptoed down rickety steps. I followed,
Willie pressed to my back tighter than honey
on corn bread.

Granny's eyes were wild when she spun around. "Lord a' mercy," she whispered. "It's a *polecat*!"

She slipped up to the kitchen . . .

. . . and came back with a raw egg swimming in a little blue bowl.

"Stay put," she ordered.

"Yes, Granny," I said.

Willie didn't say anything.

Granny crept along the wall—right toward the skunk!

I held my breath as she slowly drew him up the wide steps leading to the yard. Up . . . and up . . . and up.

Behind me, Willie twitched.

Before I could grab him, he was off the steps and racing across the cellar, waving his arms and shouting.

"GET OUT, YOU OLE POLECAT! OUT! OUT! OUT!"

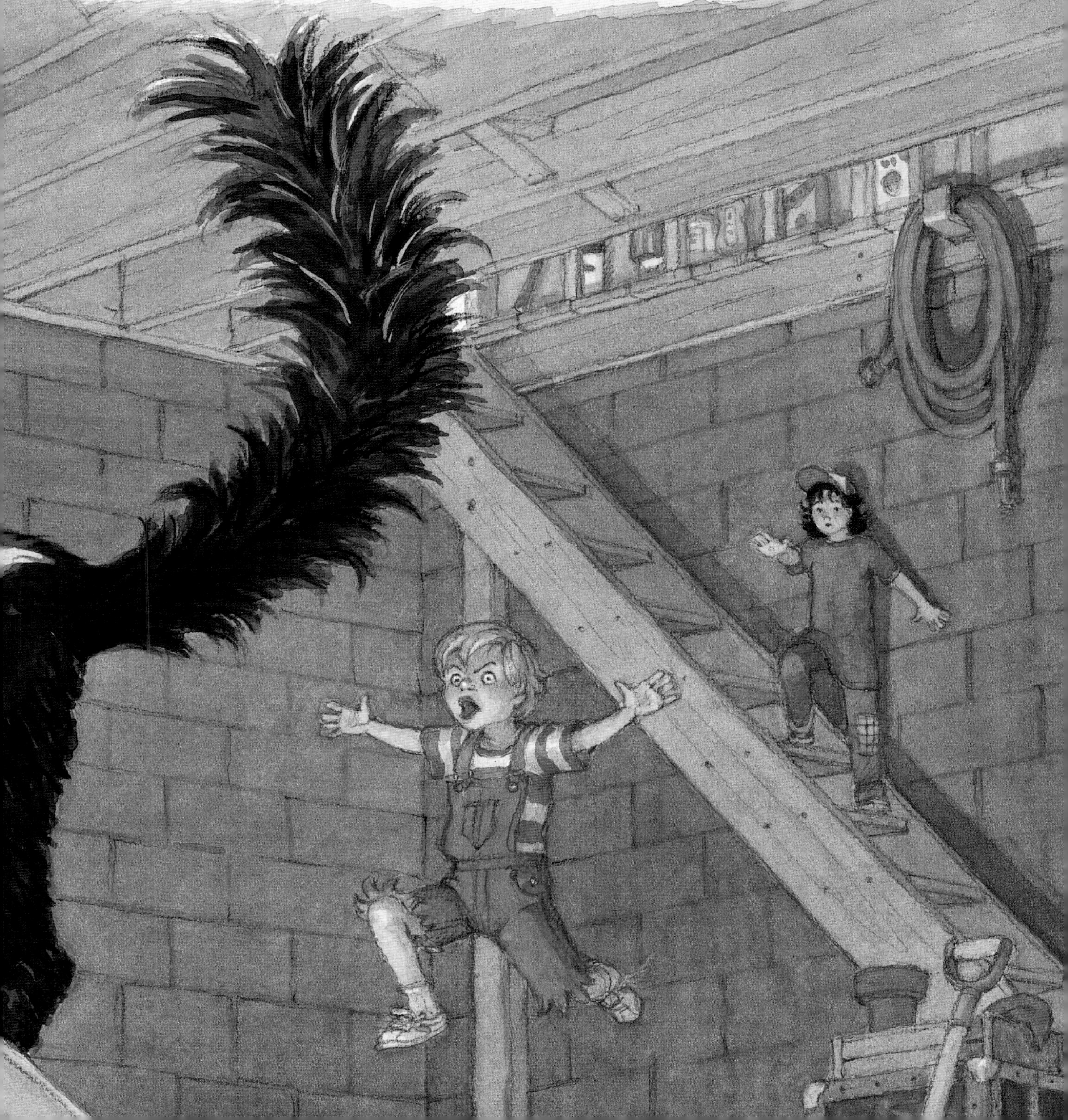

A horrible stink curled my toes and burned my nose. Hooooooo-WEE!
Willie exploded out of that cellar like a rocket—with Granny hot
on his heels.

By the time I hit the porch, that skunk was hightailing it into the
cornfield. And . . . ya-hoo! Granny had Willie by one ear, marching him
to the woodshed and calling him "ya orn'ry little dickens."

It was quite a while before Willie and Granny came back to the
house. Willie was rubbing his backside, so I knew it wasn't another hug
Granny'd given him.

The house stunk something awful—and so did we. Granny fitted us with clothespins. Said stink soup was the only thing in the whole world could rid a body of polecat smell. Said soon as she got a batch mixed up, we'd all have to jump into a tubful and scrub, scrub, scrub.

"What's stink soup?" I asked.

Granny eyed the countertops sadly. "Tomato juice, mostly." She sighed real big. "Prob'ly take every jar, too."

"Every jar?" I gave my brother the evil eye. "We did all that work for *nothing*?"

"I don't want to take a bath in tomato juice!" Willie wailed.

Wallowing in tomato juice didn't sound like a picnic to me, either, but it was better than smelling like a skunk. Besides, while Granny was explaining things to Willie again, it hit me: if we used all the tomato juice for our baths . . .

. . . there wouldn't be one red lick left for me to drink!